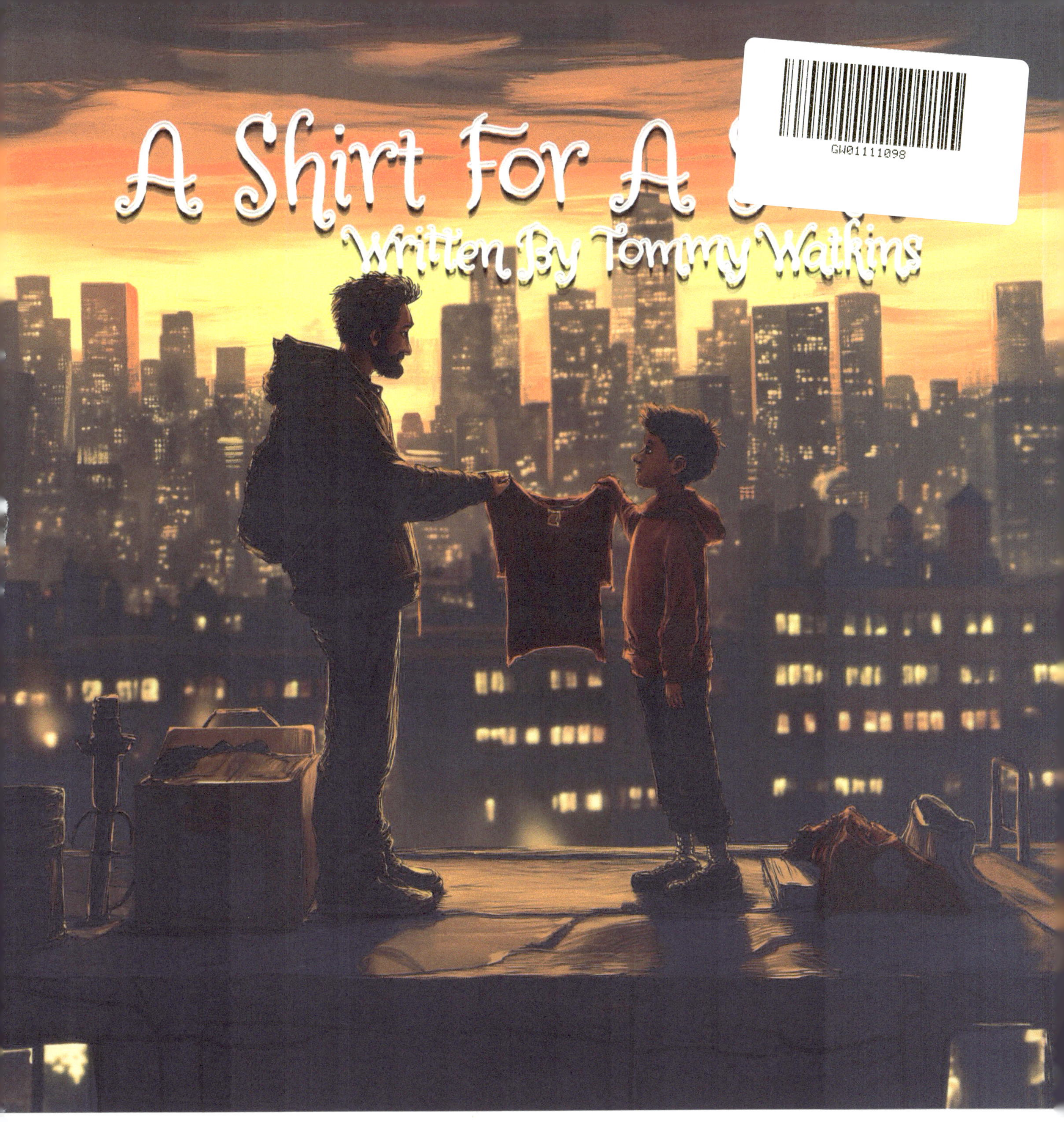
A Shirt For A
Written By Tommy Watkins

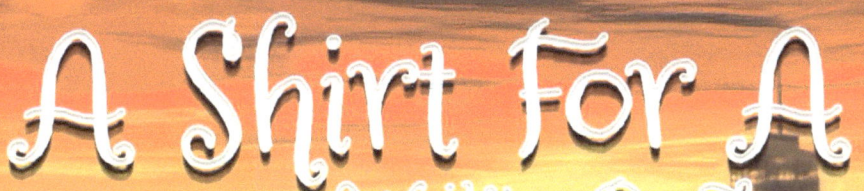

It's 7 am, the beginning of a new day

I head to the store to run some errands.

On my way, I see a man with no shirt on.

I feel sad and grab my heart in sorrow, but I feel padding. Under my clothes was a T-Shirt big enough to fit the man! I give the man the T-shirt.

On my way to the next errand, I see another woman with no socks.

Feeling under my sleeves, I find socks. I hand the woman socks and receive a gratifying smile.

On my way to the last place I go, I find a child. The child had pants on that were all ripped up.

I feel my pants and pull out another pair of pants! The child received the pants and was filled with gratitude.

The day ended with all the extra clothes given out to people. All given out to people in need; for a smile that could brighten anyone's day.

The End

Milton Keynes UK
Ingram Content Group UK Ltd.
UKHW050828170824
446999UK00017BC/3